BABY BADGER

Also by Hannah Shaw

KITTEN LADY'S BIG BOOK
OF LITTLE KITTENS

Adventures in Fosterland series
EMMETT AND JEZ
SUPER SPINACH

KITTEN LADY
HANNAH SHAW

Adventures in FOSTERLAND

Illustrated by
BEV JOHNSON

BABY BADGER

Aladdin
New York   London   Toronto   Sydney   New Delhi

ALADDIN
An imprint of Simon & Schuster Children's Publishing Division
1230 Avenue of the Americas, New York, New York 10020
First Aladdin hardcover edition January 2023
Copyright © 2023 by Kitten Lady, LLC
Also available in an Aladdin paperback edition.
All rights reserved, including the right of reproduction in whole or in part in any form.
ALADDIN and related logo are registered trademarks of Simon & Schuster, Inc.
For information about special discounts for bulk purchases, please contact
Simon & Schuster Special Sales at 1-866-506-1949 or business@simonandschuster.com.
The Simon & Schuster Speakers Bureau can bring authors to your live event. For more
information or to book an event contact the Simon & Schuster Speakers Bureau
at 1-866-248-3049 or visit our website at www.simonspeakers.com.
Designed by Tiara Iandiorio
The illustrations for this book were rendered digitally.
The text of this book was set in Banda.
Manufactured in the United States of America 1222 FFG
2 4 6 8 10 9 7 5 3 1
Library of Congress Cataloging-in-Publication Data
Names: Shaw, Hannah René, 1987- author. | Johnson, Bev, illustrator.
Title: Baby Badger / by Hannah Shaw ; illustrated by Bev Johnson.
Description: First Aladdin edition. | New York : Aladdin, 2023. |
Series: Adventures in Fosterland | Summary: Saved from a snowstorm, Baby Badger,
a newborn kitten with no mom, is taken to Fosterland, where he meets lots of new
animals, including a mama cat and her kittens.
Identifiers: LCCN 2022041604 (print) | LCCN 2022041605 (ebook) |
ISBN 9781665925556 (pbk) | ISBN 9781665925563 (hc) | ISBN 9781665925570 (ebook)
Subjects: CYAC: Foster care of animals—Fiction. | Cats—Fiction. | Animals—Infancy—
Fiction. | LCGFT: Novels.
Classification: LCC PZ7.1.S4935 Bab 2023 (print) | LCC PZ7.1.S4935 (ebook) |
DDC [Fic]—dc23
LC record available at https://lccn.loc.gov/2022041604
LC ebook record available at https://lccn.loc.gov/2022041605

To the friends we choose

as family

Contents

CHAPTER 1

A Cold, Dark World

*W*hoosh. A gust of freezing air blew through the streets, filling the alley with sparkly snow.

It seemed that everyone was hurrying inside to escape the winter storm that evening. The squirrels were hiding in their tree nests, the rabbits were fast asleep in their dens, and the pigeons were all cuddled together under the roof of the train station. The city was so still that the only sound was the whistle of the wind and one tiny squeak.

"Squeak."

Mama Mouse was still out in the cold, but she was in a hurry, gathering bits of bread from the dumpster behind a restaurant for her and her son to carry back into the hidey-hole of some unsuspecting human's attic.

The mice scurried along the edge of the dumpster, their arms filled with discarded crusts. "Listen, Mama!" the young mouse called out over the sound of garbage bags rustling in the wind. "Do you hear that?"

"Squeak."

Mama Mouse paused, and then they both shimmied down the side of the bin to seek the source of the sound. There, beside the dumpster, lay a tiny frozen kitten named Badger.

"What is he, Mama? Is he a mouse?" asked the son.

Mama Mouse sniffed the trembling baby with her wiggly nose and jumped back. "We have to go now. Come along."

Baby Badger tried to cry out for help, but all he could muster was another small squeak.

"But we can't leave him! Can't we bring him to the attic? He can share my bread crumbs. . . . ," said the son, lingering behind as his mom kept moving.

Mama Mouse turned around and gently nuzzled her concerned son. "Oh, my boy. That is no mouse. He may be our size, but that frosty being is a baby cat. And I'm afraid bread crumbs are *not* the food of choice for cats! No, no, this city will freeze over before I start inviting felines into our hidey-hole, tiny or not."

The son looked back at the creature and frowned. "But, Mama, he'll freeze."

"Kittens belong with cats—and I'm sure his family is around here somewhere," she said, pulling her son along the path.

"I feel sorry for him," said the son, and as he scooted away on the icy street, he left a trail of bread crumbs behind in hopes that it would help the mama cat find him.

To think that a mouse could take pity on a cat! *That* should tell you the danger that Baby Badger—a newborn kitten no bigger than a snowball, all alone in a winter storm—was in. He couldn't hear the wind, as his ears were still folded shut. He couldn't see the snow, as his eyes were still closed. All he could sense was a light over-head, where a bright neon sign buzzed in the dark. He tried to scoot closer for warmth, but the sign was too far away and impossible to reach. All he could do was wish to be closer to its light.

"Squeak? Squeak?" he tried one last time, but he was losing strength and couldn't muster words. As he huddled under the light of the neon star, his voice was fading into a silent whimper.

"Squeak. . . ."

For a moment, the alley was quiet

again—until the distant crunch of foot-steps in the snow drew near. Then a human bundled in scarves and gloves emerged from around the corner, fol-lowing along the mysterious path of the bread crumbs.

CHAPTER 2

The Secret Clubhouse

At first, everything was a dark, cold blur. With numb limbs and closed eyes, Badger couldn't tell left from right or up from down. The world moved all around him, but the tiny kitten stayed chilled to the bone and completely confused.

Eventually, he felt a tingling in his toe beans. *Wiggle-wiggle.* He began to move his paws. Next, he felt a tin-gling in his tail. *Wiggle-wiggle.* His tail moved side to side. His body felt like pins and needles as it began to thaw. While melting icicles dripped from his fur, a sense of relief melted over him.

He tried to use his voice. "Mama?" he squeaked hoarsely. "I think the storm is over!"

Spinning in a circle, he pawed at the soft, squishy blanket underneath him. The snow beneath his feet had van-ished, but the ground felt nothing like the hard pavement he was used to. "That's odd. . . . ," he noted.

Badger sniffed the air, which had a crisp, clean smell and was swirling with waves of warmth. It didn't smell at all like burgers and fries. He tilted his head, confused.

Nothing about this place was familiar.

"Where am I?" he said, voice cracking. Badger stretched out his arms in search of his family and felt something soft and furry. "Mama? Are you there?" But the fluffy being did not move, and its eyes felt hard like marbles.

"Sister? Are you there?" Badger nuzzled the velvety fabric of a plush toy, and it fell to its side with a *thump*.

He settled into a cozy spot in the center of a pile of plush toys and sighed. He didn't want to be on his own, but at least he was warm now.

As he drifted off to sleep, he buried his face in fluff and imagined himself surrounded by family.

That is how Badger's first days of life came and went—alone in a little warming box called an incubator, weakly wobbling about with his small plush toys and resting peacefully in the fuzzy arms of a giant stuffed teddy bear.

It's hard to know *what* is going on when you're just a baby without any ability to hear or see! But after a week in the dark, Badger's eyes began to open for the very first time, and he started making sense of the mysterious place he had landed in: Fosterland.

As his ears unfurled, Baby Badger could hear the low hum of toasty air exiting the vent. In the distance, the pitter-patter of ice against the window-pane was a faint memory of the storm. Just outside the window, wind chimes twinkled with each frosty gust, and he felt relieved to be safe and warm indoors.

As he took a first peek at the world, Badger could see the bright light above him and the glass walls that contained him in this wonderful hideaway. At his side, he saw the collection of raggedy stuffed toys that had been keeping him company: a teddy bear, a purple crocodile, and a tiny moose. He lifted his head and returned a gummy grin, happy to be in his very own clubhouse surrounded by such friendly faces.

CHAPTER 3

Imaginary Friends

"Good morning, Teddy!" Badger said, waking in the big cozy arms of the teddy bear.

"Good morning, Badger!" Badger muttered to himself, pretending to be the voice of the bear. He stretched his arms over the squishy brown fleece, which was well worn from cuddles and wash cycles, and felt right at home.

As he rubbed his eyes, he spotted the purple crocodile looking at him across the way. With bright white teeth and neon-green eyes, the crocodile always wore an eager expression, as if he were ready to whisk you away on an adventure. "*Bonjour!*" Badger said as he shot out of bed and gave him a high five. Monsieur Crocodile mostly spoke French, which Badger found very impressive.

"*Bonjour, petit chat!*" Badger responded to himself in his finest French accent.

Finally, Badger turned to Miss Moose, his tiniest and most favorite friend of all. Sitting at just two inches tall, she was even smaller than he was, and he felt like she was the little sister he'd always wanted. "Another happy day, Miss Moose!" He smiled as he groomed her antlers. "Of course, it's always a happy day with you by my side."

Ever since befriending his trio of toys, Badger hadn't felt lonely at all. He no longer worried about being separated from his feline family—the toys were the only family he needed now! They kept him company during the day, cuddled him at night, and filled his life with fun. Each had their own personality and voice (at least, they did in his mind—and that was good enough).

Aside from his plush pals, who

seemed very much alive to Badger, the only other living being he ever saw was a giant human who occasionally stopped by to feed him from a small plastic bottle. Badger referred to her as the innkeeper, because she mostly seemed to show up when it was time to change his dirty bedding or to offer him a refreshing meal.

That morning, like all the others, the incubator door slid open as the massive hand entered the friends' space. "The innkeeper is here, everyone! Special delivery! Who's ready for some breakfast?"

Badger placed his paws politely against Teddy's side and lifted his head to drink the delicious, warm formula. Eating from a bottle had become a part of his everyday routine, and he loved to lean on his friends as if they were all sharing a meal together. He could almost hear Miss Moose slurping by his side and Monsieur Crocodile calling out, "*Bon appétit!*"

After the meal, the innkeeper slid the window shut to enclose him in his living quarters, but this didn't bother him one bit. In fact, he preferred not to stray from the eyesight of his fluffy friends or wander away from the safety of his clubhouse. Weighing only half a pound, Badger thought the space was quite large enough for a little guy like him, and so the world beyond the window barely interested him.

With breakfast out of the way, Badger was full of energy and ready for fun. Lucky for him, his plush pals always seemed to be interested in the *exact* same things he was!

"Let's have a race!" Badger said, and lined everyone up on one side of the incubator to see who could make it to the other side fastest. "On your mark . . . get set . . . go!" Badger's tail stood straight up as he stepped one clumsy foot in front of the other, stumbling his way to the other side. "You can't catch me!"

Finally, he touched the wall, turned

around, and squealed, "I won!" He took a bow as the others silently cheered. His pals hadn't moved very far . . . but it was probably because he was just so speedy!

"You sure are fast!" shouted the teddy bear.

Badger held his head high. It felt good to be in first place!

"How about some acrobatics?" he said. "I've been practicing my somersaults. . . ." He rolled around the arena like a tumbleweed in the breeze. With all his rolling about, he was so dizzy that he couldn't even see if the others were tumbling, too. He collided with Miss Moose and erupted into laughter.

Just when he was feeling happy and

at ease, he caught a glimpse of a threatening presence behind him. From the corner of his eye, he could see that someone long and fuzzy was sneaking up on him!

"Eep!" cried Miss Moose. "Badger, look out—it's a snake! Save us!"

Badger yelled at the top of his lungs. "A snake?!" He did a spin-pounce, with his mouth wide open, his first tiny teeth peeking out from the front of his pink gums. "Gotcha!" he yelled, but when he spun around, the snake had just narrowly escaped.

"Come on, *petit chat*, you've got this!" Monsieur Crocodile shouted.

Badger's paws tapped about

wildly as he tried his best to capture the intruder. Twisting his body in an attempt to finally nab the black snake, he fell onto his back like an overturned beetle and flailed about with his little feet kicking in the air. Hovering just above his exposed tummy, the snake was taunting him. "Aha! Now I've got you right where I want you!"

Badger batted at his tail, eventually biting down on the furry tip with an enthusiastic *chomp!*

"*Très bien!*" said the crocodile. "You are very brave!"

Feeling quite proud of himself, Badger took a bow. Life was good.

That evening, Badger settled in for

bed, lying with his back against his Teddy. He'd had such a fun day, but with each nightfall he couldn't help but feel a little afraid of the dark. It reminded him of being alone.

With Miss Moose at his side, he gazed up at the blackness above and leaned in with a whisper. "I didn't like being alone."

"You're not alone now, Baby Badger! I'm right by your side. We're your best friends," Miss Moose seemed to reply. "And you know something? Maybe the world isn't really so dark. Maybe all you have to do is adjust your eyes. . . ."

Badger blinked a few times and slowly realized that a soft light was pouring

in through the glass of the incubator.
Outside the window, stars were flicker-
ing in the distance like glitter in the sky.
"Whoa," Badger said in a hushed voice.
"The stars . . . they're beautiful! I wish I
could pull them closer."

He extended a paw to the window,

but they were too far for him to reach.

"Even though they're far away, they're always here to light the way," Miss Moose said, her kind face illuminated by starlight. "A little glimmer of hope in the distance."

CHAPTER 4

Paw Prints in the Snow

As Badger and his plush pals dreamed about the stars, outside, the snow continued to pour from the sky like powdered sugar dumped from a bag. The entire neighborhood was coated in a fluffy blanket of white now, and just outside the window, a trail of paw prints dotted the sidewalk. At the front of the trail was Mia, a cat with a belly so round that it drooped like a giant beach ball, dragging through the snow as she ran. She had black-and-white fur, long white whiskers, and kind green eyes that scanned the windows of the houses as she passed by, searching for someone to take her in.

Long ago, Mia had been a house cat with many feline friends. Back then, she knew only the warm, comforting feeling of companionship and soft beds, but curiosity had gotten the best of her when she slinked out through an open window. Since then, she'd wandered through the town in search of adventure and now found herself stuck in a blizzard and on her own.

Well, she wasn't *exactly* on her own. Inside her belly, she could feel tiny paws tapping against her as if to say, "Hi, Mama! We're coming any day!" Mia counted the kicks and tried to guess how many babies were inside. *Two? Three? Twelve?* With how active they were, there was no telling! All she knew was that a kitten born in a snowstorm might not stand a chance, and she had to get her family to safety—fast.

She peeked into the window of a brick house. Inside, she could see a large tree in the living room, wrapped up in tiny twinkling lights. "If a tree can find refuge indoors, surely we can, too," she said as she looked down at her belly, shivering. She scratched at the door, but no one answered.

Next she tried a little yellow house. Through the glass door, she saw that a human family was sitting down for a meal together. She dreamed of meal-time by the warmth of the fireplace, but as she tapped on the windowpane, the people couldn't hear her over the crackling of the logs or the sound of their dinner conversation.

The third house she tried was a white bungalow with a wraparound porch. She stepped under the over-hang, shook off the snowflakes, and hopped up into the window. On the other side of the glass, she saw a shiny black cat sleeping on the windowsill. "A cat!" she whispered happily.

She pawed at the window, but the cat kept on sleeping. She tried again, this time scratching gently at the glass with her claws. "I'm sorry to wake you," she said, "but might you have a

vacancy? It's cold outside, and, well . . ."
She looked down at her giant belly.

The black cat blinked awake, lifted her head, and gazed at Mia.

"Please?" Mia begged, but the cat jumped down and disappeared from sight.

Mia hung her head and prepared to walk away. As she turned her back to the house, she heard the wind chimes overhead twinkling with a gust of frozen wind and felt her tummy thumping. Just as she placed a paw onto the snowy steps, she heard a creak behind her.

The door had opened wide, and in the doorway, the black cat was sitting at the feet of a human. "Come inside," the cat said. "We have room for you." Mia's tail shook with joy and relief, and she stepped inside, melting snow dripping from her fur.

A welcoming hand reached down to greet her, and the black cat bowed her head. "I'm Coco. Welcome to Fosterland. You will be safe and warm here."

Mia cried with happiness. "How can I ever thank you?"

Coco smiled. "Don't you worry. Helping cats is what we do here! Now, let me show you to your room."

She led Mia to a doorway, which opened into a cozy area complete with everything a cat could need: soft beds, blanket piles, and stacks of canned cat food! She walked around, looking high and low as she explored her new space. Now that she was safe inside, Mia could feel her motherly instincts starting to kick in. She stepped into a squishy cat bed and exclaimed with glee, "I can hardly wait to cuddle with my babies!"

Just then, Mia looked across the room and noticed a table with a curious glass-front box on top. Wanting to investigate each nook of the nursery, she leapt as high as she could and gasped as she peered inside.

CHAPTER 5

Cats Don't Need Cats

From inside the incubator, Badger heard a loud *thud*. He looked to Miss Moose. "What was that?"

"I'm sure it's just the wind," said the moose.

"Probably just the snow falling," said the teddy bear.

"Oh, my . . . it's a baby!" said a voice he didn't recognize.

Badger froze in fear. The words hadn't come from his mouth . . . or even from his mind! The fur on his back puffed up as he looked around. On the other side of the window, a giant animal was looking down at him. And she wasn't made out of plush!

"Eep!" Badger leapt into the air and scuttled underneath Teddy in terror. He may have been brave when it came to fake snakes, but the first sight of a real live cat made him tremble! The stuffed animal shook like an earthquake as he tried to hide. "Go away. I . . . umm . . . I don't want visitors!" he yelled.

"But are you alone?" she asked in a concerned tone. "Why, you're just a baby. Babies shouldn't be alone. Would you like to come lie with me? I've just found the most comfortable bed. . . ."

Badger's head popped out from under the fluffy toy. Frowning, he said, "I am *not* just a baby! I'll have you know that I happen to be a *very* independent young cat!" Couldn't she see that he was managing just fine on his own with his moose, teddy, and crocodile for company?

"I beg your pardon," said the cat in a gentle tone. "I see now that you're quite grown."

"And I'm *not* alone!" He grabbed his stuffed moose and huffed.

Mia tilted her head. "I see. But . . .

cats need cats. Don't you want to be with other cats?"

Badger held on to his moose tightly, trembling. "Cats *don't* need cats," Badger grumbled. "Not *this* cat, at least. I've come this far without them, and I certainly don't need them now." He looked at Mia and let out a soft hiss.

Mia sighed, seeing that he was quite unwilling to accept her company. "Why must you be so cold, little one?"

If only she knew how cold I've really been, Badger thought. He furrowed his brow and tried his best to send her on her way. "Please . . . just go." And with that, he popped underneath the teddy bear and vanished.

Mia looked into the incubator with warm eyes. Despite Badger's attitude toward her, she felt herself beaming with motherly love and wished she could hold him in her furry arms. She took a deep breath and softly sang:

"Little cats are meant to be
With feline friends and
family.
Alone, this world can feel
So dark and frozen.
Warming up takes time, I
know,
But someday you will melt
like snow
And know that you are
loved
And you are chosen."

Badger listened from his hiding spot. Her voice was like a lullaby, and he'd never been sung to sleep in his life. But he just shook his head. "I'm plenty warm," Badger said, his voice muffled by the stuffed animal. "I'm *literally* in a heated room. But thanks for your advice, whoever you are."

Mia smiled. "I'm Mia. I'm Mama Mia."

CHAPTER 6

Multiplying

Badger awoke the next day to the sound of a giant *thump!* He sat up in his bed quickly and looked over at Teddy. "Is that cat still out there?"

Cautiously peeking over the edge of his clubhouse door, he could see that Mia was indeed still in the nursery and was knocking over the laundry basket and dragging blankets into the corner of the room. "What is she even doing in there?" he wondered aloud as she pitter-pattered around. He pulled Miss Moose close, and together they spied on the strange new cat.

Badger wasn't interested in having another housemate—he already had his stuffed friends, and that was enough for him! But it seemed that he'd gotten one nonetheless, and she was making herself right at home. Although he didn't want to interact with her, it *was* fascinating to watch her from a distance, and Badger found himself gazing at her through the glass like a child glued to a television screen.

There was a lot about Mia that made

Badger scratch his head. For one, she seemed to be obsessed with home decorating and was creating a nest at the edge of the room. And then there was the fact that her stomach looked positively plump. As she tested out her new blanket pile, her fuzzy belly stuck out as if she'd swallowed an entire watermelon.

"Have you ever seen a cat with such a spherical shape?" he whispered to the stuffed moose and paused. "I wonder what that's all about. Do you think she's getting double portions from the innkeeper?" He stretched his neck to look down on her bowl of kibble, and as he leaned in, his head tapped against the glass, catching Mia's attention.

Mia looked up from her blanket throne and waved.

"Ack!" Badger ducked under the incubator window to hide. He did *not* want anything to do with this new neighbor! His heart was pounding as he remembered that glass is clear in both directions and that she could see him, too.

"Now just . . . stay very quiet . . . and very still . . . ," he whispered to Miss Moose, who did as Badger said. Together, they sat perfectly frozen for minutes on end until, in his stillness, Badger began to doze off. Cuddling against his moose friend, he took a long nap until suddenly . . .

"Squeak!"

Badger's paw twitched as he batted at a fuzzy mouse in his dream.

"Squeak! Squeak!"

He opened his eyes to realize the sound of muffled squeals wasn't coming from his dreams. Badger glanced at Miss Moose. "Did you say something?" he said in a hushed tone. She was silent, but the squeals continued, and he looked to the others. "Teddy, was that you?" If the noise wasn't coming from inside the incubator, then that must mean . . .

With great caution, he oh-so-slowly

peeked into the glass and saw something he couldn't believe: Mia was lying in the bed with a tiny kitten who was even smaller than he was!

"Am I still asleep?! This isn't possible!" He shook his head vigorously. "Miss Moose—pinch me!"

Miss Moose sat with her feet in the air, and Badger realized that his request was a little out of the question for a moose with hooves. "No worries, I'll pinch myself!" he said, reaching across his body and poking a claw into his own arm.

"Ow!" Now that he was feeling more awake, he hoped that the mysterious kitten would be gone. But as he peered through the glass, he saw that now there wasn't just one kitten. . . . There were *two!*

Badger rubbed his eyes. "Am I seeing double?" He turned to Teddy. "Do you see two kittens out there?"

Teddy gave Badger a reassuring smile. He was always so comforting! "No, I don't see two kittens," he seemed to say.

"Phew!" Badger said, but when he looked back . . . there were *three!*

"Huh?! How the . . . ?" He closed his eyes tightly. "They seem to be appearing out of nowhere, like a rabbit pulled out of a hat."

"Perhaps this is some kind of

magique!" Monsieur Crocodile suggested. "Try a disappearing act, *mon ami!*"

Badger wasn't sure if he knew how to do any magic tricks, but in a desperate attempt, he held a blanket in front of the window. "For my next trick . . . I will . . . make three kittens vanish! Abracadabra!" he called out, imagining that they might poof into thin air. But when he lowered the blanket, there were *four!*

Badger shrieked in shock! Had he said the wrong words? He wanted fewer kittens . . . not more!

"This can't be happening. Why are they multiplying?" he cried as he shook

the moose with all his might. He wished he could turn back time to when it was just him and his plush friends. "Isn't there anything I can do?"

"You're a great acrobat," Miss Moose said. "Maybe if you spin around, you'll turn back the clock and it'll just be us."

Badger held Miss Moose in his arms, and together they twirled in a tight circle until they bumped dizzily into the crocodile. "*Excusez moi*," he apologized.

Badger and the moose nervously peered over the glass, and to his surprise, Mia had flipped over and the four little kittens were nowhere in sight.

"We did it!" he said, hugging his

moose friend tightly. "We made the four little kittens disappear!" But Miss Moose just stared back at him with big, round eyes.

"Why are you giving me that look?" he asked the stuffed toy, but she just continued to stare. "Don't tell me . . ." He slowly turned to the window and looked back at the blanket.

Mia had turned over, revealing that the kittens had reappeared—and now there were *five*.

CHAPTER 7

Kitten Safari

Badger was not happy about the new arrivals. For the rest of the day, he stared at them, grumbling at the realization that they were not going to be disappearing anytime soon. "This is the worst," Badger huffed.

"*Au contraire,*" the crocodile seemed to suggest. "Perhaps this is the start of an adventure! Why, this could be . . . a kitten safari!"

"A kitten safari?" Badger raised an eyebrow.

"*Oui, oui!* This could be *très magnifique!* Who knows what dangers lie ahead—or what mysteries will unfold!"

Badger let Monsieur Crocodile's idea sink in. *A kitten safari . . . that could be fun!*

He stood up straight, fixed his whiskers, and tipped his nonexistent hat at the toys to welcome them to the beginning of their tour.

"Plushies and gentlefluff, are you ready for a wild ride? Today I'll be taking you on . . . a kitten safari! That's right, today you'll be observing these wild wiggleworms in their natural habitat. But don't worry, you'll be safe behind this protective glass barrier. Please keep your arms, legs, and antlers inside the vehicle at all times. And now . . . we're off!"

He held his paw to his brow, gazing into the corner at the blanket nest. He leaned in and instructed his passengers to observe the kittens. "Well, folks, here you can see a big cat surrounded by a bunch of really little ones who are doing some kind of . . . odd activity. Hmm . . ." He scratched his head as he observed the babies suckling and kneading. What *were* they doing, after all? "Yes, what you are observing is . . . uh . . . well, the babies are digging for some kind of . . . tummy treasure!"

"*Mon Dieu!*" shouted the crocodile. "What curious creatures!"

"Yes, yes, they're very peculiar, aren't they?" Badger nodded. "And such a variety of colors, too. There's stripes, spots, and . . . I must say, that one looks like a peanut butter chocolate brownie!"

"I love peanut butter brownies," peeped the moose.

"Aha! And it looks like Mia the big cat likes them, too. Why, she's licking that brownie-swirl kitten all over! Everyone, watch as this enormous cat licks the little one's face . . . and back . . . and . . . ew!" Badger gasped and hid behind the stuffed bear in horror. "Is Mia *licking that baby's butt*?!"

All the stuffed animals seemed to giggle as Badger stuck out his tongue in disgust. "Why would she do that!?

Ick, ick, ick!" He rolled on the incubator floor, laughing with them until he had tears in his eyes. Mia did such weird things! Eventually, he caught his breath and said, "Nature is wild, you guys."

As Badger got back into character, he saw that the kittens were writhing around the blanket nest, clumsily scooting and squirming without direction. Soon, a little gray one had wiggled too far from the others and was calling out in thunderous cries louder than a fire alarm. "Here we have a wandering screamer. I suppose he doesn't like being alone," he said, pausing in momentary reflection. "But the silly guy can't see that the others are *right there,* just within his reach."

Mia shot up and ran over to scoop up the screamer with her mouth. The kitten dangled contentedly from her teeth as she carried him back to the nest, and Badger felt a pang of longing in his heart. "Oh . . . she's their mom," he realized. He thought back to when he'd been lost and alone, crying out for help—but his mom hadn't been able to locate him, and his siblings were nowhere to be found. It seemed like these babies had it much easier: a warm bed to sleep in and someone to find them if they ever should stray.

He tried to put it out of his mind. If he'd learned anything in his first weeks of life, it was that he did *not* need other cats.

"Everyone needs someone to lean on," Teddy said in a comforting tone. (He always seemed to know what to say.) "That's why you have us!"

Badger fell into the squishy bear, leaned against the crocodile, and hugged the moose. "You're right. I love you guys!"

For days, Badger went on observing the kittens like this and trying to learn about their ways. They seemed to live as one unit, lying in massive cuddle piles with all their legs and arms entangled like a knot. As for Mia, she never seemed to leave their side, except to use the litter box or scarf down some food. She spent most of her time lying on the blanket, gazing at the babies and kneading the air.

As far as Badger could tell, the kittens' eyes were closed, and they couldn't see him observing them. To be sure, he would make funny faces and stick his tongue out at them as Mia napped. "They have no idea we're here!" he laughed to his toys.

But one day, something changed. He looked down at the blanket nest for his daily safari and saw a pair of tiny peepers looking right back at him.

"Psst! Hey! You! What are you doing up there?" It was the peanut butter brownie kitten.

Badger hid behind the crocodile. He didn't want to talk with another kitten!

"I know you're in there. . . . I can still see your whiskers!" the kitten called up.

Badger shouted out in the voice of the crocodile, "*Je ne parles pas chat!*" (Which translates to: "I do not speak cat!")

The kitten laughed. "You're hilarious! Are you pretending to be a stuffed animal?"

Badger stepped from behind the toy with a furrowed brow. "I'm not pretending! That's my friend Monsieur Crocodile. He's French."

"Are you for real? That's gotta be the coolest thing I've ever heard!" said the kitten. "Well, pleased to meet you, Monsieur Crocodile. I'm Leeni!" She turned to Badger. "And you are?"

Badger choked

up. He had never had a conversation with a kitten before. "I'm . . . I'm Badger."

"I've gotta know. How on earth did you befriend a crocodile from France? It must be a fascinating tale!"

Badger scratched his head. *She thinks I'm the fascinating one?* His heart was pounding as he tried to figure out how much to share. Should he tell her all about the winter storm and how he nearly froze solid? Should he tell her about the chill in his bones and the way his stuffed animals saved him? No, no, it was all too much—and she was a stranger. She could never understand. He looked at the crocodile and said, "We go way back. . . . It's a long story."

"And what about that weird box? What are you doing in there?"

Badger was confused. He'd spent so much time looking out from the window that he had never considered what his life looked like from the outside in. To Badger, the incubator was his home, and everything else was unknown. To Leeni, the incubator was a mystery.

"This is my clubhouse. It's where I live."

"Do you ever get lonely in there?"

Badger shook his head from side to side. "I have three wonderful friends.

And I ought to be getting back to them now. So long." He slid down low between the teddy bear and the moose—a safe space for him to hide away.

CHAPTER 8

An Invitation to Lunch

Ever since Leeni noticed Badger, his secret clubhouse didn't feel secret at all. All day, she interrupted his play-time with the plush toys and tried to find ways to get his attention. "Psst!" she called as she tossed a piece of kibble up at the incubator window. "Hey, you!"

Badger peeked over the edge, a bit frazzled. "Yes?"

"Want to join us for a meal?"

Badger looked to the toys.

"An invitation!" whispered Monsieur Crocodile. "An adventure, *mon ami*!"

Badger's heart was pounding. "I . . . I don't think so. I already have lunch plans."

"With who? Your plush friends? Do they even eat?" Leeni scratched her head.

Badger turned back to the toys and paused, realizing he'd never *actually* seen them eat food. Still, the thought of leaving the clubhouse—and interacting with other kittens—was terrifying!

Leeni begged. "Come on! It'll be fun. You can meet my whole family. Besides,

I see you watching us all the time! Why not join us?"

"We'll be right here when you get back," Teddy quietly encouraged him.

Badger sighed. It *could* be interesting to observe the kittens close-up, but he was a little scared of what it would be like to interact with real live cats . . . and so many of them. What if he didn't fit in?

"You should go," he heard Miss Moose whisper. "You're a great guy. They'll love you."

"Well?" Leeni smiled. "Will you come?"

"I guess so," Badger said hesitantly. "When is lunch?"

Leeni laughed. "What do you mean? We eat pretty much all day! Breakfast, lunch, dinner—it's all just one long meal that never ends. Come down anytime!" With a toothless grin, she waved good-bye and went back to the blanket pile with the others.

Badger turned back around, and the toys all seemed to cheer. "Here goes nothing!" Badger said, unsure.

Looking through the glass, he'd always felt like he was watching a television show . . . but now he was invited to step through the screen! He took a deep breath and began contemplating the daunting task of exiting the incubator for the very first time.

"Hnnnnngh!" He strained as he nudged the glass, trying to see if he could open it.

Pop! It cracked open slightly, and he felt a gust of cool air against his face. He shot back, afraid of exiting the warm safety of his bedroom. What if the rest of the world was just as cold as the storm had been? He winced at the thought as he reached a paw out of the crack to test the air, then cautiously stuck his head through the gap.

"Nope! Can't do it," he said to himself, but it was too late. In all his wiggling at the incubator door, he'd lost his balance and tumbled downward, writing and hollering, and landed clumsily on a pile of blankets below with a tremendous *flop!*

"Badger! You came!" Leeni squealed.

"That was . . . quite an entrance." A

chunky gray kitten laughed to the others, who all broke out in giggles.

"Hush. Be nice," Mia whispered to her babies. She turned to Badger. "Welcome, Badger. How lovely to have you here! Come, sit with us."

Badger sidestepped toward them, nervously looking around as ten tiny eyes stared back at him. He took a deep breath. There was no going back now.

CHAPTER 9

The Odd One Out

Mia gestured toward the new arrival. "Everyone, meet Badger. Go on . . . introduce yourselves, little ones."

A stripy girl lifted her head. "I'm Anya Lasagna."

"Big Tony," said a big gray boy with white paws. "And this is my pal Lil Macaroni—"

"But you can call me Mac," said a kitten who looked just like Tony but smaller.

"I'm Rizzo. Nice to meet you," a striped boy chimed in.

Leeni scooted to the side to make room for Badger. "You already know me, of course!" she said. "I saved you a spot at the milk bar."

Badger stepped closer, his hair still fluffed and rather disheveled. He tried to think of something normal to say. "Thanks for the invitation. . . . I sure am hungry."

"Us kittens are always hungry!" Anya shouted. "Dig in!" And with that, she lowered her face against Mia's tummy and started to suckle.

Badger looked around, confused. He didn't see anything to eat. "Thanks. Umm . . . where's the food?"

Big Tony turned to Mac and cackled. "This guy thinks he's a real jokester, eh? 'Where's the food?' That's hilarious!"

Badger giggled along but had no idea what was so funny. He felt like he must be missing something! "Do you know when lunch will arrive?"

Anya momentarily unlatched. "It's *always* lunchtime at the milk bar, silly."

Badger took a closer look and gasped. "There's food *in there*?"

Big Tony chimed in: "Yeah, if you can manage to find a good seat! Anya here's always taking the best spot." He shot a glance at her, clearly annoyed. "But hey, wiggle your way in there and try for yourself! Nothing tastes better than a homemade meal from your mama, am I right?"

Badger looked at Mia's belly and felt overwhelmed. He wasn't used to this family dynamic at all, and the thought just made him feel out of place and uncomfortable. "Umm. I'm sure it's delicious, really. And I totally would. It's just . . . I don't think . . ."

Just then, the door creaked open and a pair of feet stepped past the kittens. Badger craned his neck to see the innkeeper now standing at the open incubator with his warm bottle, looking confused. "I'm down here!" he meowed, and she turned to him with a shocked look on her face, surprised to see that he was now sitting by Mia's tail.

The innkeeper kneeled down and patted Badger on the head, seeming to approve of his escape. She extended a hand and offered him his bottle, and he felt very relieved to have a meal that made sense to him.

"Ah, *here's* my lunch!" he said, and began to drink from the small bottle filled with formula.

The kittens all stopped their suckling. As Badger blissfully chugged, the others tilted their heads and watched him in total bewilderment. They had never seen something so strange! Once the bottle was empty, he licked the last bits as formula dripped from his chin and let out a satisfied belch. *Burp!* "Oops. Um. Pardon me."

"What the heck was that?" Big Tony asked. "Why do you drink from that . . . weird plastic thing?"

Badger felt awkward. "What do you mean? That's just my lunchtime bottle."

"What's in it?" Rizzo asked, with his face scrunched in confusion.

"It's like a warm, creamy liquid. . . . It tastes good," Badger said.

"I don't get it. Why doesn't it come from a mama?" Mac asked with a puzzled look. "Where *is* your mama anyway?"

Badger looked down at his paws. He didn't know how to answer.

"Mac, don't be rude!" Leeni interjected. "Kittens eat in many different ways."

"But if he doesn't have a mama . . . who grooms him? How can he keep his coat clean and neat?" Rizzo asked, sniffing the air. "Now that I think about it, he does smell kind of different."

"He doesn't have the family scent," Big Tony agreed.

Badger had never heard of such a thing in his life. "What's a family scent?" he muttered.

"It's how we know who belongs," said Mac.

"Boys, that's quite enough!" Mia interrupted. "Badger, excuse them. A family scent is simply a familiar smell that cats have in common when they live together as a group." She turned back to the kittens. "I'll have you know, little ones, that Badger only smells different because he's probably had a more interesting life than any of you can imagine! You smell like the safety of this nest . . . but Badger smells like adventure."

"Adventure?" Big Tony raised an eyebrow. His mom was right—he'd never stepped a paw out of his blanket nest. "Tell me more!"

Badger didn't know what to say. It was true that he'd been through a lot, but how could he begin to explain all of that to these kittens? They could never understand his life on the street or what it was like to grow up as an orphan whose role models were all stuffed with cotton!

For a moment, Badger sat in silence, shifting nervously on his paws, until Leeni spoke up. "Badger is friends with a crocodile."

The kittens all looked at him. "Is that true?" Rizzo asked.

"And a bear, and a moose, too," Badger said, and the others gasped in amazement. And while he was glad they were taking an interest in him, deep down, he felt that their curiosity was just making him more like an outsider. He didn't fit in with them at all.

"Anyway, I'd better get going now," he said, turning his back.

"Won't you stay and be our friend? We want to hear about your adventures!" Leeni begged.

But Badger had made up his mind. "Thanks for having me," he said, and started his journey back to his secret clubhouse: clawing his way up the side of a laundry basket, climbing up cases of cat food, and leaping from blanket stack to blanket stack to make it to the top.

"Are you sure you don't need a helping paw?" Mia called up to him.

Badger looked down and said, "Thanks, but I don't need help from other cats. I can do it on my own." He leapt to the top of the table, stepped back inside his incubator, and took a deep breath.

"You won't believe the day I had," he said as he laid his head on Teddy and wrapped his paws around Miss Moose. The toys sat quietly as he told them how awkward he had felt at his first kitten luncheon. "Thank you for listening, friends. I never feel like the odd one out with you."

CHAPTER 10

Hide-and-Seek

*S*mack! *Smack, smack, smack!* Badger awoke to the sudden sounds of pieces of kibble banging against his window. He looked out of the clubhouse to see all the kittens staring up at him.

"Wanna come play with us?" Leeni said, and the others echoed her.

"Yeah! Come be our friend!" Anya shouted.

Badger closed his eyes. What kind of friend wakes you up when you're fast asleep? Miss Moose would never do such a thing! Plush friends are always peaceful, but it seemed that the kittens were determined to give him a headache.

Smack! They just wouldn't stop with the kibble! Badger turned to Miss Moose and grumbled, "They are relentless." But Miss Moose just smiled an encouraging smile, and so he rubbed his eyes and looked over the edge again. "Okay, I'll be right down."

As Badger slipped out of the incubator to join them, he caught a glimpse of his reflection in the glass. His hair was messy from sleeping pressed against the teddy bear, and he licked his paw and tried his best to tame his mane. After fussing with it for a few moments, he shrugged. It wasn't perfect, but it would have to do.

"You're here!" the kittens squealed as Badger arrived. Their coats looked clean and neat, all slicked back from being freshly licked by their mama. Badger hoped they didn't notice his bedhead or think he smelled too strange.

"We were just about to play our *favorite* game," Leeni said. "It's called hide-and-seek! We'll hide, and you have to try to find us."

Badger nodded. That sounded fun!

He closed his eyes and counted to ten, then looked around and all the kittens were gone. He chuckled, remembering when he'd longed for them to vanish as babies. And he felt funny realizing that now he kind of liked having them around . . . just a little!

"I'm coming for you!" he called out.

Badger peered around the room. The empty tissue box on the table looked a little odd, like there were two ears poking out from the top. He leapt up and tapped the top, and Rizzo popped out from it like a jack-in-the-box!

Next, he noticed eight white paws sticking out from underneath the curtain. "Gotcha!" he called out as he slid the curtain to the side, and Mac and Tony laughed as they were found.

Hmm. He looked around and noticed that the cat bed was vibrating. As he got closer, he could hear little giggles coming from underneath. "I hear you under there!" he shouted, and Anya jumped out, cracking herself up.

Where was Leeni? He looked under blankets, in cabinets, and behind the litter box, but she was nowhere to be seen. Just then, he looked to the stack of supplies and screamed.

"The snake!"

Badger pounced as fast as he could

to catch the fuzzy black snake, which was sticking out from a cardboard cat food box.

Leeni jumped out from the box, and the snake moved behind her. "Leeni, there's a snake on you! Don't worry, I'll help you!" The two kittens somersaulted around the room, completely entangled together, until they hit the door with a *thud*.

Leeni laughed profusely, finally getting out the words: "Badger, that's my tail—it's part of me!"

Badger paused and looked at Leeni and saw that it was indeed attached to her body. "You have one, too," she said.

Badger looked behind him and laughed. "So I do! Just like yours." The two of them were out of breath from their wrestling and grinning from ear to ear.

"Okay, I'll go next," Anya said, and she

began to count to ten. Badger was so excited to hide! He darted around the room, then settled into a fantastic hiding spot in the cabinet. From inside, he peeked through the crack of the door and saw the other kittens hiding—Rizzo was in a cardboard cat carrier, Leeni was hiding in a blanket pile, and Mac and Tony were sitting very still inside the laundry basket.

Anya began to sniff around the room. She walked right past the cat carrier, calling out, "I'm coming for you!" without noticing her brother.

She sniffed around the blanket pile. "Come out, come out, wherever you are!" she said, not noticing her sister.

She stood next to the laundry basket, smelling the air deeply. Four little eyes peeked out at her through the holes, but it was like she couldn't even see them!

With her nose on the ground, she slowly worked her way toward Badger, and his heart pounded. He held his breath as she stepped closer and took a whiff of the cabinet door.

"Gotcha!" she shouted, and pulled the cabinet door open to reveal that Badger was inside.

Badger laughed. "How'd you know? I was hidden so well!"

"The nose knows." Anya winked, and with those three words, Badger felt his heart sink into his stomach. He realized then that he had lost the game because he was different—he stood out from the others because he didn't have the family scent. He was a misfit.

A rush of emotions hit him, and he didn't want to play anymore. He began to walk back toward his clubhouse with a lump in his throat.

"Are you leaving?" Anya asked. "But we're still playing! I haven't even found the others yet. . . ."

"I've got to get going now," Badger replied.

Mac and Tony popped their heads out over the edge of the laundry basket, and Rizzo jumped out of the carrier.

"But we love playing with you! Won't you stay?"

Badger swallowed his sadness. "I don't think so," he said, climbing the supply stack to head back to his safe space.

Leeni popped her head out from under the blanket pile and looked at him longingly. "But—" Leeni started, but Badger interrupted her.

"It's fine. You guys play your family game. I'm okay on my own."

CHAPTER 11

Under the Stars

That night, Badger lay in his incubator with Miss Moose, staring at the ceiling. After the day he'd had, his mind was spinning, and he wasn't sure where he belonged anymore. It felt like the whole room was dark again—and he was lost.

"Look to the stars," Miss Moose seemed to say.

He looked out into the room, where Mia and the babies were fast asleep together. It was a normal night in Fosterland.

But then Badger noticed something different.

Not only was the room lit by the stars in the sky, but there seemed to be a bright, twinkling glow coming from the nursery door. He thought back to his carefree playtime with Leeni and realized that in all their tumbling, they'd serendipitously cracked open a door that had previously stayed closed. He sat, mesmerized, wondering what lay on the other side.

"Maybe hope is closer than you think," Miss Moose said.

Curiosity bubbled up inside him. He looked to his plush friend and asked, "Are you thinking what I'm thinking?"

He gently held the tiny moose between his teeth and slipped out of the clubhouse, tiptoeing past the snoring kitten pile as he made his way across the room.

Badger placed his paw against the door, and it quietly creaked open, giving him a first glance at the living room of Fosterland. "Whoa," he said as he saw the most magical thing he had ever laid eyes on: a gigantic tree

covered in little twinkly lights and colorful balls.

He stretched his neck back as far as it would go and set his sights on the tippy-top of the tree, where a huge golden star was shining brightly.

For a moment, he sat there, taking in the view. More than anything, he wanted that star.

"We've got to climb to the top!" he said. "If we could just get that star, we could put it in the clubhouse . . . and then it would never feel dark ever again! Think we can do it?" He reached for the bottom branch, but it was too high.

He lifted Miss Moose over his head. "Can you reach?" He tossed her upward, and although she touched the branch, she flopped immediately to the floor with her hooves in the air. "Ah, right. The hooves."

The two sat under the tree, looking up at the twinkling lights, and Badger sighed. "It's so close . . . but so far."

"I believe in you, Badger. I know you can reach that star," Miss Moose said. "You just might need help from someone else."

Badger felt a small sting in his chest. All his life, Miss Moose had been his best friend, but she was right—she might not be cut out for this particular adventure. "That's okay," he said, and tried to think about who else he knew who might be good at climbing. "Maybe we can try again with Teddy and Monsieur Crocodile tomorrow night."

As he creaked the door to the nursery open and snuck past the kittens with the moose in his mouth, he noticed Leeni's ear begin to twitch. She peeked with one eye and whispered, "Badger? What are you doing awake?"

"Shh. Forget you ever saw us," he replied with a hushed voice, and hopped back up to rest in his clubhouse.

The next evening, when all was quiet, Badger tried again. He gently tossed each of the plush toys from the incubator, trying not to wake Mia and the sleeping kittens, and dragged them out to the living room. Standing under the sparkling tree with his three plush friends, he stared at the star above and was entranced.

"Teddy, you're a bear. Surely you can climb to the top and get the star!" he said eagerly.

Teddy just sat still.

"Well, can't you?" He scooted the teddy bear underneath the first branch, but he didn't climb. "Don't you want to help me?"

Teddy smiled. "Of course we all want to help you. We all love you. It's just—"

"Monsieur Crocodile, how about you? You're an adventurous one! Can't crocodiles climb?"

"*Mais oui*," he started. "Crocodiles can surely climb trees. There is just one *petit* problem. . . ."

Badger felt his throat tightening. He just wanted to climb to the star! He turned to Miss Moose, who was sitting very still, and lifted her to his face. "Why won't anyone help me?" He squeezed her tightly and cried into her fabric fur, which sopped up his tears. Along her back, he noticed that a small thread was coming loose, and all at once it hit him.

"We love you, Badger, but you're growing up now. You need friends who can do more than just snuggle. You need friends who can play—who can help you climb a tree. You need friends who are more than just fabric and fluff," he heard Miss Moose say.

Badger took a deep breath. Just fabric and fluff? He didn't want to hear it.

"Maybe cats *do* need other cats," Miss Moose said, and Badger winced. He didn't want to admit that she might be right.

"No. I can do this on my own."

He stared upward, gazing at his reflection in a low-hanging glass ball. "I can do this." With a courageous butt-wiggle, he took a leap of faith to grab hold of the ornament overhead.

Bam! The ornament hit the ground with a smash, and he jolted back.

Suddenly, he heard a voice whispering from the doorway. "Badger? What are you doing out here?" In all the commotion, Leeni had stirred once more from her slumber. She rubbed her eyes in confusion. "What . . . what is this amazing thing?"

"Don't worry about it. It's nothing. It's . . . ," Badger said, but then he saw that Leeni was just as amazed as he was. "Well . . . it's a star-covered tree, I suppose."

"But how did you find this? You're incredible!" she said. "You really are an adventurer!"

"The door must have popped open yesterday when we were tumbling. I noticed the glimmer, and . . . here it is. I've been trying to figure out how to get to the very top."

"Alone?" she asked.

"Well, not exactly alone, but . . ." He looked at his plush pals. "It turns out that my friends here aren't so good at climbing."

Leeni was glowing in the multicolored light, little speckles of red and green shining in her eyes as she looked right at him. Tilting her head, she said, "Why do you *really* want to get to the top?"

Badger paused, then pointed up. "I just need to get to that star."

Leeni nodded and sat next to Badger, settling onto a gift wrapped with

checkered paper. Badger climbed onto
a gift of his own, and for the first time
he felt like he might be bonding with
another cat. He leaned back and looked
up at the star above.

"The truth is . . . I've been afraid of the dark since I was a baby," Badger admitted. "When I was little, I was stuck in a snowstorm, and everything was black—and freezing cold. I was alone, and it was scary. But I could sense that there was a light overhead . . . and I thought if I could just touch it . . . just move closer . . . everything might be all right. I guess I've always seen stars as a sign of hope."

Leeni leaned in, listening.

"A star is a source of warmth in the cold. A source of light in the dark! And for the first time in my life, it's close enough that I can almost touch it. Maybe this is my chance to finally find that light and warmth I've always wanted."

Leeni's eyes welled with tears. "That's beautiful, Badger."

"Also," he added, "to tell you the truth, I really just have an urge to knock it off the top of the tree."

"O-M-G. I get the urge to knock stuff over, too!" Leeni squealed.

"You do?"

"I do! Do you ever see a pen on a table and just think . . . 'I want that to be on the floor'?" Leeni batted at the air and laughed.

"Ha ha! I do! Wow, I didn't realize we had so much in common," Badger said.

Leeni looked at Badger with a

comforting grin. "Did we just become best friends?"

Badger nodded. His heart tingled like the feeling he'd had when warming up from the storm. He was thawing.

"But how am I going to get up there?" He sighed as he turned his attention back to the star. "Turns out my friends are made of fluff, and they can't help me make it to the top."

"Maybe *they* can't," Leeni replied. "But I think I know a whole bunch of kittens who can. . . ."

CHAPTER 12

Secret Meeting

As the sun began to rise, the two kittens snuck back into the nursery and slipped into their separate beds. Leeni settled back into the kitten pile and fell fast asleep while Badger lay awake in his incubator, buzzing with excitement from his evening with his new friend. He stared at the ceiling, plotting their adventure, until he couldn't keep his eyes open any longer.

Soon the other kittens woke up for the day, but Leeni felt so tired that she didn't even stir. She slept through the sounds of paws scratching in the litter box, jingle-balls rolling across the floor, and even the clink of cat food bowls as breakfast was delivered.

Mama Mia licked her on the head. "Are you feeling okay? Why are you so sleepy?"

"I'm okay, Mama," Leeni said. "I just needed a few more minutes of rest."

Leeni finally got up and slinked over to the food dishes, where her siblings nibbled and slurped up breakfast. After checking to ensure that her mama wasn't listening, she whispered to the others, "Secret meeting. Badger's clubhouse. Ten minutes."

The kittens' ears perked up. They looked to each other and nodded in excitement. "Finally, an adventure!" Mac squealed.

As Mia settled in for a morning siesta, the kittens climbed the makeshift staircase of boxes and blanket stacks, heading toward Badger's secret clubhouse. Now that they were growing bigger, they could make it all the way to the top of the table for the very first time, and they marched proudly one after another into the unknown.

Badger slid open the incubator door, and his heart pounded as each kitten entered, all in a line. It was the first time any living being aside from him had set paw inside his room, and the realization that *he* was hosting *them* made him excited . . . and a little proud!

They huddled in a circle and kept their voices low, trying not to wake up Mia.

"Okay, gang. You wanted an adventure . . . ," Leeni started, and the kittens nodded. "Well, Badger has an idea—and it's going to take all of us to make it happen."

Badger cleared his throat. He had

never had so many eyes on him at once! "We've discovered something incredible. A marvel. A wonder of the world!"

The kittens' eyes widened.

"A tree so tall, you can barely see the top—all aglow with twinkling lights like the night sky. And at the tippy-top: a golden star. The mission . . ." He paused. "*Our* mission is to make it to the highest point and retrieve that star."

"A quest!" Mac peeped.

Outside the incubator, Mia pretended not to hear their planning. But mothers can hear their wee ones from a mile away, and she secretly listened in on every low-mumbled word.

"At the stroke of midnight, we

convene at the portal to the rest of Fosterland," Badger said in a serious tone.

Rizzo tilted his head. "At when, we do what, where?"

Badger sighed; the kittens didn't understand his adventure-speak. "What I'm saying is that tonight, after the innkeeper has turned off all the lights and gone to bed, and Mama Mia has closed her eyes, we're going to meet up by the nursery door."

"Got it!" Rizzo said, holding a paw to his head in a salute.

Badger already had a plan. "Mac and Tony, you're the muscles. Your job is to move the gift boxes into position so that we can reach the tree and climb."

"You got it!" they said in unison.

"Rizzo and Anya . . . you're our lookouts. Your job is to watch out for any motion from Mama Mia or the innkeeper. If either of them catch on to what we're doing, we'll never get the star."

Rizzo and Anya nodded. "Understood!"

"Miss Moose, Monsieur Crocodile, Teddy, your very important job is to act as a decoy," he said, looking at the plush toys. He turned to the kittens and explained, "We're going to stuff them under the blankets so it looks like you're all still in bed."

"That's genius!" Tony snickered.

"And, Leeni—you and I are going to climb."

"Yeah, we are!" Leeni said, offering up a high five.

Badger touched paws with her and felt a burst of warmth inside. It was so cool that everyone wanted to help him with his plan!

Badger ended the meeting and cracked open the incubator door. "See you tonight . . . team."

Thinking they were *very* sneaky, the kittens tiptoed down from the incubator and past their mama, who acted as if she were just waking from her nap. They resumed the day as usual: enjoying a midday snack, grooming one another on the blanket pile, playing with tunnels and balls, and soaking up the sunny spot on the floor as it moved across the room until eventually the sun set and disappeared.

That evening, they would set out on their adventure.

CHAPTER 13

The Climb

"Shh," Leeni whispered as Rizzo, Tony, and Mac dragged the stuffed animals across the floor in the darkness of night. "Stack them in the cat bed."

Anya laid a blanket over the top of the bed and giggled. It looked just like they were all asleep under the fleece. "She'll never notice we're gone!"

The five pitter-pattered toward the
door, where Badger was waiting for
them, making final calculations about
how he would get to the top. Under the
light of the tree, he was trembling with
nerves and excitement. Leeni stood at

his side and gazed up at the star with him. "We've got this."

In a hushed voice, Badger said, "Welcome, everyone! Today we are embarking on a daring feat—one that many kittens have attempted in their lifetime but only the fiercest felines could dream to complete. Are you with me?"

"Yeah!" the kittens whispered excitedly, and they each began to help in their own way.

Mac and Tony lifted gift boxes and stacked them atop one another, working together to form a stairway that reached the branches.

Anya stepped to the top and picked up a little golden bell that was hanging on a branch, saying, "This can be our alert system!" Rizzo untied a ribbon from a gift, threaded it through the bell, and the two took their positions at the doorways, each holding the end of the ribbon.

Leeni grabbed on to a tinsel garland and ran in circles around the tree until it unraveled. Tugging at it, she called over to Badger. "I think it can hold our weight!"

Badger pulled on the tinsel and smiled. "We're ready for our ascent."

"If anything happens . . . ," Mac said, "Tony and I will break your fall with this pillow."

"Good luck!" Anya whispered, and Rizzo gave a thumbs-up.

Standing atop a glittery box, Badger stepped out onto the first branch, holding on tight to the tinsel rope. "Well, friends . . . up we go!"

Just behind him, Leeni grabbed a

branch and said, "Let's get your star."

Up, up, up! The two were up and away, through the pine needles and past the glass orbs, picking up bits of glitter on their fur as they went. Down below, the kittens cheered them on: "You've got this!"

Badger spotted a little figurine of a bird dangling on the edge of a branch. "Hey, Leeni, check this out!" he said as he swiped it with his paw, and it went flying off the tree and onto the floor. All the kittens cracked up—Leeni most of all.

"Okay, watch me!" Leeni lifted her paw high, then smacked at a candy cane until it flew across the room.

Badger was laughing so hard that he couldn't even hear the creak of footsteps across the house.

Rizzo's ears shot to the side. "The innkeeper!" he shrieked, and began to shake the ribbon with all his might, causing the bell to ring.

"Everyone hide!" Anya called out, and slid underneath the tree skirt with the ribbon and the bell.

Mac and Tony hopped behind the boxes, and Tony plopped a red bow on top of Mac's head.

Rizzo stood tall between two nutcrackers, pretending to be a decorative statue.

Up in the treetop, Badger and Leeni

slipped into the pine branches, with only their faces visible. They sat very still as the innkeeper stepped out of the bedroom to head to the kitchen for a glass of water.

Badger tried to do his best impression of an ornament, and as the innkeeper walked sleepily past the tree and went back into her bedroom without noticing him, he was delighted.

"All that hide-and-seek paid off," Leeni said as the kittens all came out from their hiding spaces. "Way to go, gang!"

As he and Leeni neared the tippy-top, Badger's heart was pounding in excitement. "Leeni, we're so high up!

Look at us—we're doing it! We're almost to the star!"

Leeni smiled and said, "That's what friends are for."

Badger held on tightly to the tinsel with one hand, and with the other, he began to reach upward. He could feel the heat of the star warming his fur. But just as Leeni took her final step up the branches, she slipped.

"Ahh! Help!" she yelled as she dangled in the air, holding on to a branch tightly. Beneath her, her feet wiggled as she struggled to find her footing.

Badger was so close to the star, but his friend needed him. He whipped his head downward, pulling his paw away from the star and offering it to her instead.

With Badger's help she scrambled onto the branch beside him. "Leeni! Are you okay?" he said. Between their faces, the golden star glistened.

"I'm great now!" she said. "But look, Badger . . . we made it to the star!"

Badger gazed at the star, then turned to his friend. Leeni's face was shining in its glow, her loving smile sparkling like a sunbeam directly into his heart. When he looked at her, the star didn't seem so important anymore. The only thing Badger cared about was the safety of his friend—his very best friend. A bright light washed over him, melting away his

sorrows and filling him with joy. And in that magical moment, he knew that he already had everything he needed.

"All this time I've been looking for warmth, but it was right here in front of me." He paused and looked down at the others. "You've all given me my greatest adventure of all just by welcoming me into your lives."

He wiped a tear from his eye. "The star is beautiful. But I don't need the star, Leeni. I just need love!"

"You *are* loved, Badger!" Leeni said as she reached past the star and wrapped her arms around Badger.

"We all love you, Badger!" the kittens shouted from below.

Happiness melted over him like the sunshine on a summer day, and Badger closed his eyes as he soaked it all in.

"But we're still gonna smack it down, right?" Leeni winked.

"Oh yeah. It's on!" Badger said, and together the two batted it back and forth until it tumbled to the ground. Rizzo and Anya gathered around as Mac and Tony caught the star with their decorative pillow, and as Badger and Leeni climbed downward, they knocked off every ornament they could! The kittens below batted at the fallen decorations, and as Badger and Leeni hopped down to meet them, the branches shook until all of them were absolutely covered in glitter, pine needles, and bits of tinsel.

With everyone back on the floor, they gathered around the star, all huddled together in one big group hug. It was the coziest Badger had ever felt—surrounded by fluff and friends.

CHAPTER 14

The Family Scent

The nursery door creaked open, and Mama Mia stood in the doorway. The star, the orbs, the tinsel, and nearly every decoration were strewn about the room, and the kittens were sparkling with craft glitter as they stood under the tree, shocked to have been caught.

"Are we in trouble, Mama?" Anya

asked, brushing a piece of tinsel away from her face.

The kittens gulped and stood up straight in a row, nervous to hear what Mia had to say.

Mia just sniffed a fallen ornament and smiled. "No, baby. Exploring with your friends is part of growing up."

"But . . . you aren't surprised to see us here?" Leeni asked.

Mia smirked. "Do you really think I can't tell the difference between my own babies and a couple of stuffed toys?" The kittens laughed, relieved to hear that their mama wasn't too upset.

Mia lovingly brushed away the pine needles from her daughter's face. "I'm actually very proud of you all for being so brave and for joining your friend on such an exciting escapade." She leaned in and sniffed Leeni's cheek, her nose wiggling gently. "And I must say . . . you sure smell like adventure now!"

Big Tony jumped up and down. "Ooh! What about me? Do I smell like adventure now, too?"

Mia sniffed at Tony and nodded, then turned to the six kittens, all covered in sparkles and smiling. She sniffed Anya . . . then Mac . . . then Rizzo . . . and then she leaned into Badger and inhaled deeply.

"Yes, you all smell like adventure

now. And you, my boy—you smell like family."

"I do?!" Badger asked, with big, happy eyes.

"A new family scent." Mama Mia smiled. "One with a hint of pine, glitter, adventure, and love."

Mia rubbed against the base of the tree and her tail quivered contentedly. "All right, my little ones—let's go home."

The six kittens pranced back to the nursery, their paws skipping past piles of ornaments. Leeni kicked one sideways as they passed, and Badger kicked it right back to her. Oh, how wonderful it felt to be part of a real cat family!

As they entered the room, the kittens hopped into bed with the little plush toys. Badger stood back, looking at all of them—everyone he had ever loved in his life—and dived right into the middle.

Badger spun in a semicircle next to Leeni, and as he laid his head on her side, he heard a low, rumbling purr. Like a chain reaction from one to the next, he noticed each kitten begin to vibrate. *Purr-purr-purr.* Even though he knew that his stuffed friends weren't truly alive and couldn't hear it, he hoped that they could somehow sense the happiness of that moment, and he imagined that if they could, they would be very proud of him.

Mama Mia leaned over to groom her babies with long, wet licks, their fur slicking back with each stroke. For the first time, Badger felt her sandpaper tongue brush through his hair. *So this is what it's like to be loved,* he thought.

Badger took a deep breath, and as he exhaled, he felt a rumble escape his throat, adding to the family chorus. A symphony of purrs!

From that moment on, Badger spent every waking moment with the kittens. He never felt cold or afraid, because he always had someone to snuggle. And he never felt lonesome, because now he had the family scent—and he knew he belonged.

CHAPTER 15

Chosen Family

Weeks passed, and the kittens had outgrown the nursery and settled in the living room of Fosterland. Badger was big enough to hop into the windowsill now, and he sat looking out at the neighborhood, watching as the innkeeper dragged the dried-out tree to the curb.

Everything seemed to be changing. The scent of pine had gone away and was replaced with the smell of pretty pink cherry blossoms that were blooming just beyond the window screen. The snow had melted, and the sun was shining brightly. The once-chilly air was now lovely and warm, with an occasional gentle breeze that swept past the wind chimes, twinkling a happy song.

Badger had changed, too. His baby-blue eyes were now a soft aqua-green, and he had long, lanky legs and a silky-smooth coat. Looking out the window at the changing seasons, he noticed the birds chirping, the squirrels leap-ing through the trees, and even a little mouse scurrying by. Badger tapped the window with his paw, and the little critter paused, looking up at him with a grin as if he recognized him from somewhere, then hurried away.

Badger knew there was a life outside of Fosterland, and as he looked out the window and listened to his foster friends chatting on the living room couch, he wondered what adventures might lie ahead for him beyond the front door.

"I can't wait to go to Foreverland!" Big Tony said to his mama. "I bet there are even more adventures to be had there!"

"A lifetime of adventure," Mia said.

"And cat trees bigger than you can even imagine . . . ones that you *will* be allowed to climb. . . ."

"Don't you worry about leaving your family?" Badger said, revealing that he was feeling a little anxious about their graduation from foster care. "Don't you worry about being alone?"

Tony paused. "I don't think so. I've never been alone, and if Foreverland is as awesome as they say it is, then I doubt I'll ever have to be. Everyone knows: cats need cats!"

Badger laid his head down on his paws. "It's hard for me not to worry about being alone again," he admitted.

Mama Mia hopped up into the

window and put a loving paw on Badger's back. "I know how you feel. Believe it or not, I can understand. Did you know before coming here I was outside in that same snowstorm as you?"

"You were?" Badger looked up at her with disbelief.

"I was. And I didn't like being alone either. But then I came to Fosterland, and I found you, Badger. I felt that you were family from the moment I saw you! In a way, you were my first baby. And now here we are, a big happy family, ready for our happily ever after."

Mia petted Badger on the head and continued. "We can't change the past, but we can choose our future."

Jingle-jingle. Leeni walked into the room wearing something around her neck and hopped up onto the windowsill with Badger and Mama Mia. Badger extended a paw and touched the silver tag. "What's this?"

"I have some exciting news." Leeni smiled. She held her head high to show off her new collar, batting at it with the flick of her paw. "Do you know what this means?"

Badger shook his head.

"It means today is adoption day!"

Badger felt his heart begin to thump. "Today?!"

He turned away from Leeni and closed his eyes tightly, trying to process that their time together in Fosterland was coming to an end. He knew that adoption was the biggest day in a kitten's life . . . but change was so scary! What if he went to a home with no other cats? What if he was alone again, with no one to talk to? Having known the love of a feline family, the thought was enough to give him the chills.

With his eyes shut, he took a deep breath and told himself that no matter what, he would be okay.

"That's wonderful," he quietly said, fluttering his eyes open and looking out the window.

Leeni lifted something to his ear.

Jingle-jingle. His ear tilted toward the sound.

"But I haven't told you the best part. . . . ," Leeni said with a smile. *Jingle-jingle.* She gently shook the object again. Badger turned his head and saw that Leeni was holding in her paw a collar identical to hers. "This is for you."

Badger's eyes opened wide. He looked at Mama Mia, then back at Leeni. "What does this mean?"

She placed the collar around his neck. "It means we're going home together, Badger! Me and you, forever!"

Badger's eyes welled with tears. "Do you mean it?! Leeni . . . this is amazing!" He leapt out of his seat and held his

paw to his collar. "But wait. You could give this collar to anyone. Why wouldn't you choose a family member?"

Leeni placed a paw on Badger's shoulder. "What do you mean, Badger? You *are* my family. Family is more than just who you're born with. Family is who you choose. And, Badger . . . I choose you!"

Their collars jingled together as they hugged each other tightly, and they looked like a perfect pair.

"This is a celebration!" Mama Mia said. "Badger, you are loved—and you are chosen!"

Badger and Leeni hopped down from the window, their collars jingling in harmony. "Congratulations!" the others shouted, and all of the kittens hugged one last time.

"If we're really leaving Fosterland, there's someone else I need to say goodbye to," Badger said, and walked to the nursery room with Leeni following behind him. There, in their old bed, the plush toys sat in a pile, looking back at him with the same smiling faces he remembered from when he was young.

"Well, everyone . . . I'm getting adopted!" He looked to Leeni. "Can you believe it? I have a family."

He placed a loving paw on the bear. "Teddy, thank you for always keeping me warm when I was cold. You showed me comfort at a time when I needed it most."

He looked to the crocodile. "Monsieur Crocodile, you always taught me to be brave. You pushed me to do new things . . . and look at me now. Thank you. Er . . . I mean . . . *merci beaucoup!*"

Finally, he picked up the moose. "Miss Moose, you showed me companionship when I felt lonely. Because of you, I learned how to love. I'll be grateful for you, always."

The three stuffed animals didn't reply. Badger giggled at himself for hoping one last time that they might.

"Do you want to bring them with you?" Leeni asked. "There should be enough room in the carrier. . . ."

Badger looked out the window and took a deep breath. "Someday, there will be more little babies like me who need comfort and warmth. And when they come here, they're going to be so lucky to have these three. I wouldn't be who I am without them." He patted them each on the head. "Thank you all for the love you showed me. If you ever miss me, remember: just look out to the stars."

Badger turned to Leeni and felt ready to leave Fosterland. The two friends took one last look at the nursery where they'd grown up together, breathed deeply, and walked out the door. In the living room, a happy couple was waiting for them with open arms. Badger and Leeni hugged tightly. "We're going to be family forever, Badger," Leeni squealed.

"A true forever family." Badger smiled, and together they walked into the carrier to make their way to Foreverland.

The True Story of Baby Badger

Baby Badger was born during a snowstorm in Mount Rainier, Maryland, just blocks from where I lived at the time. When I received a call about a little, frozen, newborn kitten whose mama had run away, I quickly warmed up a microwavable heat pad, threw on a winter coat, and hurried out the door.

When I arrived, Badger was just hours old and was completely hypothermic—

he was so cold that he was not moving at all. I placed him on top of the fleece-covered heat pad, cupped my hands over his tiny body, and vigorously rubbed his fur. Slowly he started to be able to move, and I transported him home to continue warming him up inside an incubator in my nursery room. It isn't safe to feed a cold kitten, so I waited until he had reached a comfortable body temperature to feed him his first bottle. He loved to eat and eventually started to grow from a tiny jelly bean into a sweet, young kitten.

During Badger's first weeks, he battled some health issues, like tummy troubles and megaesophagus, a condition that made it hard for him to eat comfortably. He stayed in the incubator until he was three weeks old, quarantining to make sure he was healthy before he met other cats. During that period, I took in a pregnant cat named Mama Mia from the outdoors, who gave birth mere hours after arriving. I named her kittens after pastas: Tortellini (Leeni), Lasagna (Anya), Macaroni (Mac), Rigatoni (aka Big Tony), and Risotto (Rizzo.)

Mama Mia's babies were chunky, healthy, and deeply loved by their mother. When it came time for Badger to meet them, he really didn't know what to make of other cats! He was quite awkward with them at first, but eventually he learned to accept love from Mia, and to play with the other kittens. Before I knew it, he had totally integrated with their family and no longer chose to hang out on his own. He even became friends with other kittens who arrived later on and eventually was part of a crew of *eleven* kittens!

Right away, Leeni and Badger became the best of friends. They could be found grooming each other, chasing wand toys, and even falling asleep curled up together. When it was time for adoption, Mama Mia and Anya found a home together, Mac and Tony found a home together, and Rizzo went home with a kitten named Coleslaw from another litter. But Badger and Leeni had both made it very clear: they wanted to go home together! And so, after they were spayed and neutered, they found a wonderful forever family in Washington, DC, where they still live to this day.